E   Miller, Rose.
MIL   The old barn

          92035283 /AC

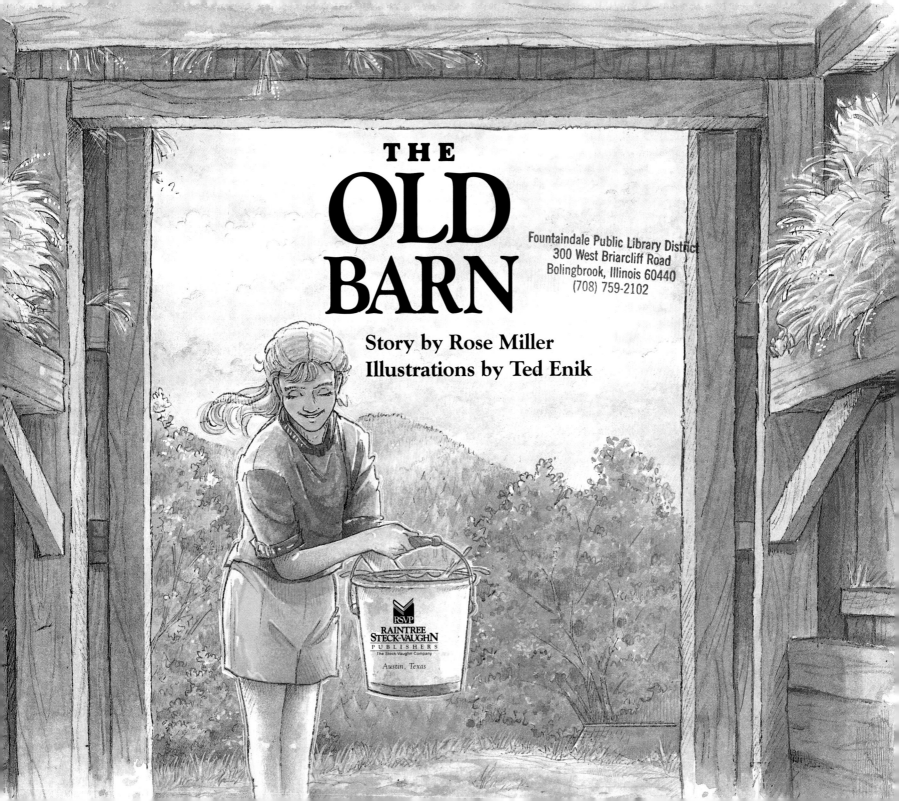

THE
OLD
BARN

Story by Rose Miller
Illustrations by Ted Enik

RSVP
RAINTREE
STECK-VAUGHN
PUBLISHERS
The Steck-Vaughn Company

Austin, Texas

I would like to thank my teacher, Lynn Black, for giving me a guiding hand whenever I needed one. I would also like to thank my friends and family for being patient whenever I was frustrated and for encouraging me to complete my work. — **R.M.**

Printed in Mexico.

1 2 3 4 5 6 7 8 9 0   RRD   97 96 95 94 93 92

Library of Congress Number: 92-35283

Library of Congress Cataloging-in-Publication Data

Miller, Rose, 1980–
　The old barn / story by Rose Miller; illustrations by Ted Enik.
　p.　cm. — (Publish-a-book)
　Summary: After her grandfather dies, Sarah's parents are in danger of losing the family farm, until Sarah remembers the story he had told her about coins buried under the old barn.
　1. Children's writings, American.　[1. Farm life — Fiction. 2. Grandfathers — Fiction.　3. Children's writings.]
I. Enik, Ted, ill.　II. Title.　III. Series.
PZ7.M63337Ol　　1993　　[Fic] — dc20　92–35283
　　　　　　　　　　　　　　　　　　　　　　CIP
ISBN 0-8114-3581-4　　　　　　　　　　　　AC

Sarah was eleven years old when her Grandfather Hutchins died. His death had caused Sarah a lot of pain. It was very hard for her to understand why this had happened to someone she needed very badly.

4

Grandfather Hutchins had always taken care of Sarah while her parents worked in the town mill on the third shift. She spent all of her extra time helping Grandfather with all the little chores that needed to be done. They spent many hours in the old barn feeding the cows, hauling hay, cleaning the stalls where the small calves slept, and tagging calves' ears.

But her favorite times were spent just listening to Grandfather tell stories about when he was a boy. The old barn was the place where they didn't disturb her parents, who had to sleep most of the day.

9

So for Sarah there was a very lonely spot in her heart as she stood in the empty barn trying to do the chores alone. As she stood there, she could close her eyes and almost hear Grandfather singing, as he always did while he worked.

Her grandfather was born in South Carolina in 1900. He was one of ten children who helped keep the sixty-acre farm clean and productive. When he was ten years old, the Hutchins family decided to build a new barn. Their new barn would be like their old barn in one way. The Hutchins family always secretly put four silver coins wrapped in a burlap bag under the right main door frame. When the old barn was torn down, the coins would be used to pay for the new barn.

The coins were like insurance to the Hutchins family, who might not always have the money to build a dependable barn. Any farmer could have a bad year and lose a barn to a bad storm. This had happened to Sarah's great-great-great-great-grandfather. So that was when the Hutchins family decided to start the family tradition of secretly placing coins under the barn frame.

No one would know this except the members of this family. And so far no strangers had tried to steal the coins. Grandfather had told her about this family tradition many times, and he always seemed so proud of it.

PAYMENT DUE:

Since Grandfather's death, the Hutchins family had more hardships. Sarah's mother and father were laid off from the mill because of something called a recession. They had looked everywhere for anything that would help pay the bills. There was not a lot of money to buy food, and her parents got behind on their mortgage of the farm.

A year before, Sarah's dad had mortgaged the farm to buy a new tractor. Now the bank was threatening to take the whole farm if the payments were not made soon.

Final Notice

When Sarah overheard her parents talking about this, she went to the barn to think. She stayed there thinking how awful it would be not to have this farm anymore. Her family had owned these sixty acres for the last one hundred and fifty years. There was a certain pride from living on land that your ancestors had bought. Sarah's family didn't have a lot of money, but it was important to them to be called a Hutchins and to live on the Hutchins's land.

19

That night as Sarah lay in bed thinking about what Grandfather might have done, she heard thunder in the distance. It began raining, and with every minute the storm seemed to be getting closer and closer. Soon the wind was roaring and whistling. Lightning was flashing on and off like a light bulb.

Then came the roar like a train, and Sarah ran to the kitchen, as did her parents. They all got under the table and waited. As quickly as it had come, the storm was gone.

Sarah's father tried to look outside, but it was too dark. He told them that they would have to check on things in the morning. Sarah really wanted to check on the old barn but decided her father was right about not being able to see much and went on to bed.

With the first light, Sarah sprang from bed, dressed, and ran outside. Tree branches and leaves were everywhere. Sarah ran up the hill to where she could see the barn. Her first glimpse was horrifying. The barn was completely gone! She ran falling and sliding down the muddy hill. When she got to the bottom, she screamed, "No!" Then she fell to the ground and cried.

After some time Sarah stopped crying because she felt something under her right knee. When she raised her knee up, she saw an old muddy burlap bag. Then she remembered the story her grandfather had told her about when he helped his father build the barn. In all of the confusion of the past months, she and her family had forgotten about the buried coins.

The story of when her grandfather and his father put four old silver coins in a burlap bag and buried them under the frame of the main door came back to her. At that moment Sarah knew that Grandfather was still watching over the Hutchins family.

The coins turned out to be very valuable. The first coin went to pay off the mortgage at the bank.

The second coin was used to help Sarah's parents start raising chickens so they could be home with her.

The third coin was used to build a new barn.

But the fourth coin was not spent.

On a very cold
morning Sarah and her father secretly
buried the old coin with three newer coins in a
burlap bag in that special hole. Later that day the
new barn would be started. The bag with the coins
would be under the frame of the main door of the
barn that soon would be built.
As Sarah finished helping her father cover the
hole, she smiled because the Hutchins's family
tradition would continue. Sarah could hardly
wait to pass the secret on to her children.

Rose Miller's story of **The Old Barn** is based on a real family tradition. Her family wasn't aware of the tradition, however, until one day when Rose saw some older people walking around on her grandfather's property. She wondered what they were doing, so she asked. They said they used to live next to her grandfather and were his good friends. They told her about his tradition of putting the coins under the barn when it was built. That gave her the idea for this story.

Rose was born in Greenville, South Carolina, on December 28, 1980. When she was a fifth grader at Keowee Elementary School in Seneca, South

Carolina, she decided to put the story of her family tradition down on paper to share with others. She was sponsored in the Publish-a-Book Contest by Lynn Black, her teacher.

Rose spends her time with her mother, Julia, in Morganton, North Carolina, with her father, Bobby Lee, in Seneca, South Carolina, and with her grandparents in Fries, Virginia. Her favorite sports are skating and swimming. She remains interested in writing and is looking for more publishers that publish books by students. She has many creative ideas for her writing projects. One of her recent stories is called "The Murderous Rocking Chair."

The twenty honorable-mention winners in the **1992 Raintree/Steck-Vaughn Publish-a-Book Contest** were Heidi Roberts of Dresden, Maine; Jessica McCulla of Mesa, Arizona; Kristine Laughlin of Mount Laurel, New Jersey; Tori Miner of Franklin, Connecticut; Brittany Kok of Decatur, Illinois; Hilary Manske of Clintonville, Wisconsin; Mandy Baldwin of Bothell, Washington; Kristin Yoshimoto of Honolulu, Hawaii; Arwen Miller of Kent, Ohio; Jessica Martin of Wauwatosa, Wisconsin; Jessa Queyrouze of Mandeville, Louisiana; Kay-Lynn Walters of Fostoria, Ohio; Karen Lauffer of Edgewater, Maryland; Karey Vaughn of Somerset, Pennsylvania; Matthew Kuzio of Mandeville, Louisiana; Leonard Ford of Germantown, Tennessee; Carolyn Hack of Overland Park, Kansas; Emily Levasseur of Hudson, New Hampshire; Christina Miller of Port Jefferson, New York; and Shawna Smith of Hays, Kansas.

Ted Enik has been a children's book illustrator long enough to have a few shelves piled with books he has worked on. When he's not up late, mole-eyed, hunched over slow-drying paint, Ted enjoys living in New York City's Chinatown with Heidi and two imaginary cats.